Have you seen Elephant?

For
Mum, Dad
and Jo

Have you seen Elephant?

David Barrow

GECKO PRESS

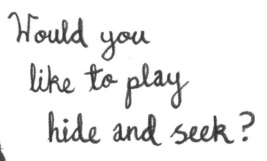

Would you
like to play
hide and seek?

OK. You hide.

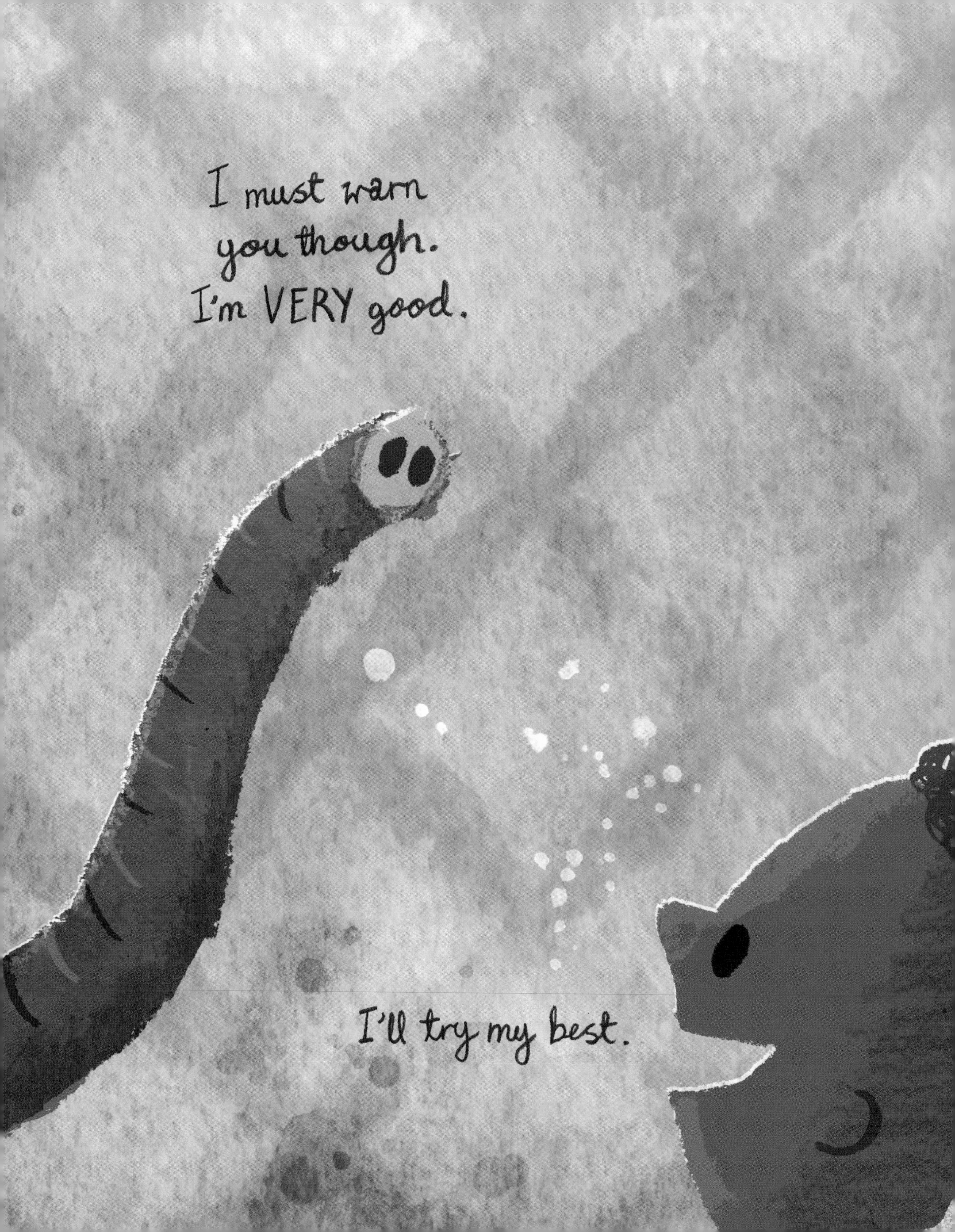
I must warn you though. I'm VERY good.
I'll try my best.

6 7 8 9

Not under here.

Maybe I'll try
outside.

I give up!

There you are!

Hey, what are you playing?
Hide and seek.

Would you like to play tag?
OK.

I must warn
you though...

... I'm VERY good!

This edition first published in 2015 by Gecko Press
PO Box 9335, Marion Square, Wellington 6141, New Zealand
info@geckopress.com

Reprinted 2016 (twice)

Distributed in New Zealand by Upstart Distribution, www.upstartpress.co.nz
Distributed in Australia by Scholastic Australia, www.scholastic.com.au
Distributed in the United Kingdom by Bounce Sales & Marketing, www.bouncemarketing.co.uk
Distributed in the United States and Canada by Lerner Publishing Group, www.lernerbooks.com

First American edition published in 2016 by Gecko Press USA, an imprint of Gecko Press Ltd
A catalog record for this book is available from the US Library of Congress

© David Barrow 2015

Designed by Vida & Luke Kelly, New Zealand
Printed in China by Everbest Printing Co Ltd, an accredited ISO 14001 & FSC certified printer

ISBN hardback: 978-1-776570-08-9
ISBN paperback: 978-1-776570-09-6
Ebook available

For more curiously good books, visit www.geckopress.com